3 4028

HARRIS COU

D1516427

JPIC Sandbu
Sandburg, Carl
Never kick a slipper at the
moon

WITHDRAWN

$16.95
ocn183179436
11/24/2008

Never Kick a Slipper at the Moon

by **CARL SANDBURG**

illustrated by

ROSANNE LITZINGER

Holiday House / New York

Text by Carl Sandburg, first published
in 1922 in *Rootabaga Stories* (New York: Harcourt,
Brace and Company)
Illustrations copyright © 2008 by Rosanne Litzinger
All Rights Reserved
Printed and Bound in Malaysia
The text typeface is Nueva.
The artwork was created with opaque and
transparent watercolors, colored pencil, ink, and gouache
on fine 140-lb cold-press watercolor paper.
www.holidayhouse.com
First Edition
1 3 5 7 9 10 8 6 4 2

Library of Congress Cataloging-in-Publication Data
Sandburg, Carl, 1878-1967.
Never kick a slipper at the moon / by Carl Sandburg ;
illustrated by Rosanne Litzinger.
p. cm.
Originally appeared in Rootabaga stories,
by Carl Sandburg in 1922.
Summary: Explains why parents in Rootabaga
Country warn their daughters not to kick their
slippers at the moon.
ISBN 978-0-8234-2160-2 (hardcover)
[1. Humorous stories.]
I. Litzinger, Rosanne, ill. II. Title.
PZ7.S1965Ne 2008
[Fic]—dc22
2007043210

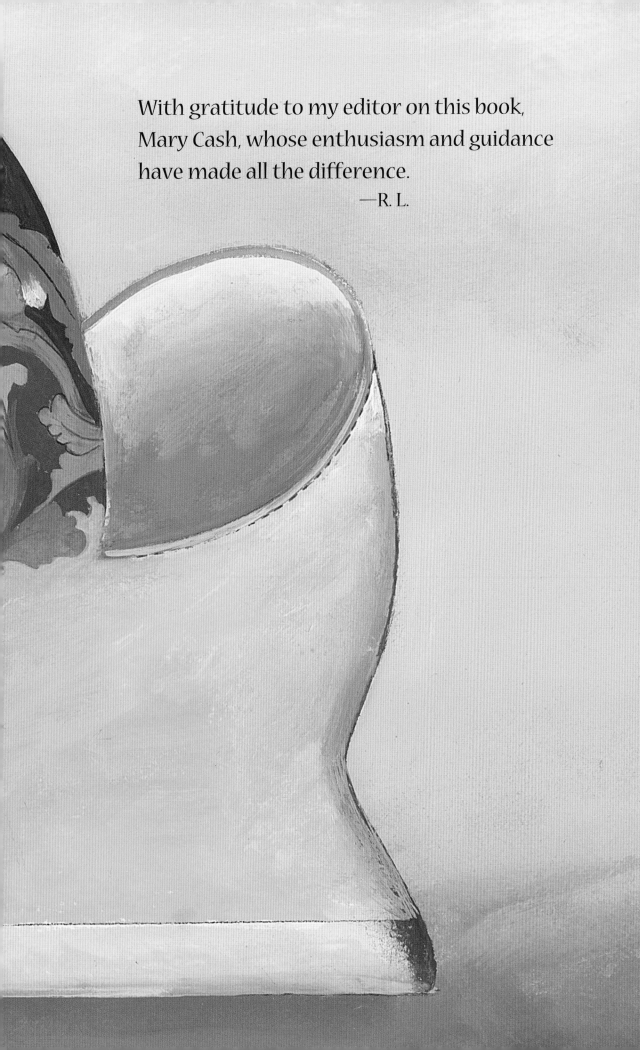

With gratitude to my editor on this book,
Mary Cash, whose enthusiasm and guidance
have made all the difference.
—R. L.

The moon
is a friend for
the lonesome
to talk to.

—*Carl Sandburg*

When a girl is growing up in the Rootabaga Country she learns some things to do, some things *not* to do.

"Never kick a slipper at the moon if it is the time for the Dancing Slipper Moon when the slim early moon looks like the toe and the heel of a dancer's foot," was the advice Mr. Wishes, the father of Peter Potato Blossom Wishes, gave to his daughter.

"Why?" she asked him.

"Because your slipper will go straight up, on and on to the moon, and fasten itself on the moon as if the moon is a foot ready for dancing," said Mr. Wishes.

"A long time ago there was one night when a secret word was passed around to all the shoes standing in the bedrooms and closets.

"The whisper of the secret was: 'To-night all the shoes and the slippers and the boots of the world are going walking without any feet in them. To-night when those who put us on their feet in the daytime are sleeping in their beds, we all get up and walk and go walking where we walk in the daytime.'

"And in the middle of the night, when the people in the beds were sleeping, the shoes and the slippers and the boots everywhere walked out of the bedrooms and the closets. Along the sidewalks on the streets, up and down stairways, along hallways, the shoes and slippers and the boots tramped and marched and stumbled.

"Some walked pussyfoot, sliding easy and soft just like people in the daytime. Some walked clumping and clumping, coming down heavy on the heels and slow on the toes, just like people in the daytime.

"Some turned their toes in and walked pigeon-toe, some spread their toes out and held their heels in, just like people in the daytime. Some ran glad and fast, some lagged slow and sorry.

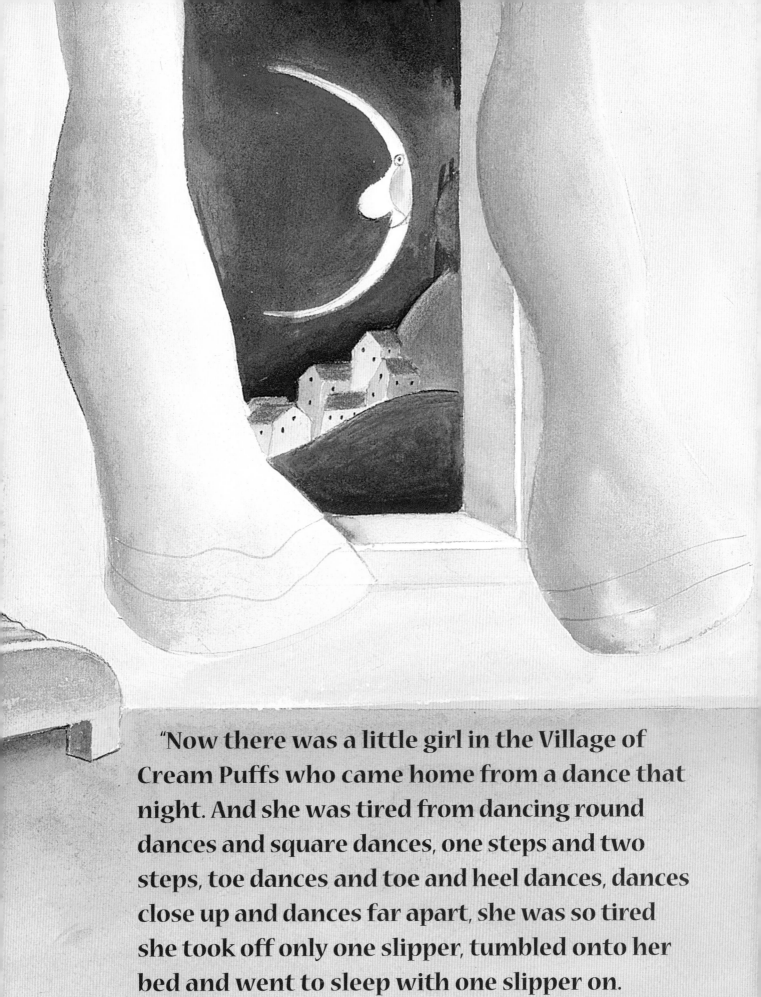

"Now there was a little girl in the Village of
Cream Puffs who came home from a dance that
night. And she was tired from dancing round
dances and square dances, one steps and two
steps, toe dances and toe and heel dances, dances
close up and dances far apart, she was so tired
she took off only one slipper, tumbled onto her
bed and went to sleep with one slipper on.

"She woke up in the morning when it was yet dark. And she went to the window and looked up in the sky and saw a Dancing Slipper Moon dancing far and high in the deep blue sea of the moon sky.

"'Oh—what a moon—what a dancing slipper of a moon!' she cried with a little song to herself.

"She opened the window, saying again, 'Oh! what a moon!'—and kicked her foot with the slipper on it straight toward the moon.

"The slipper flew off and flew up and went on and on and up and up in the moonshine.

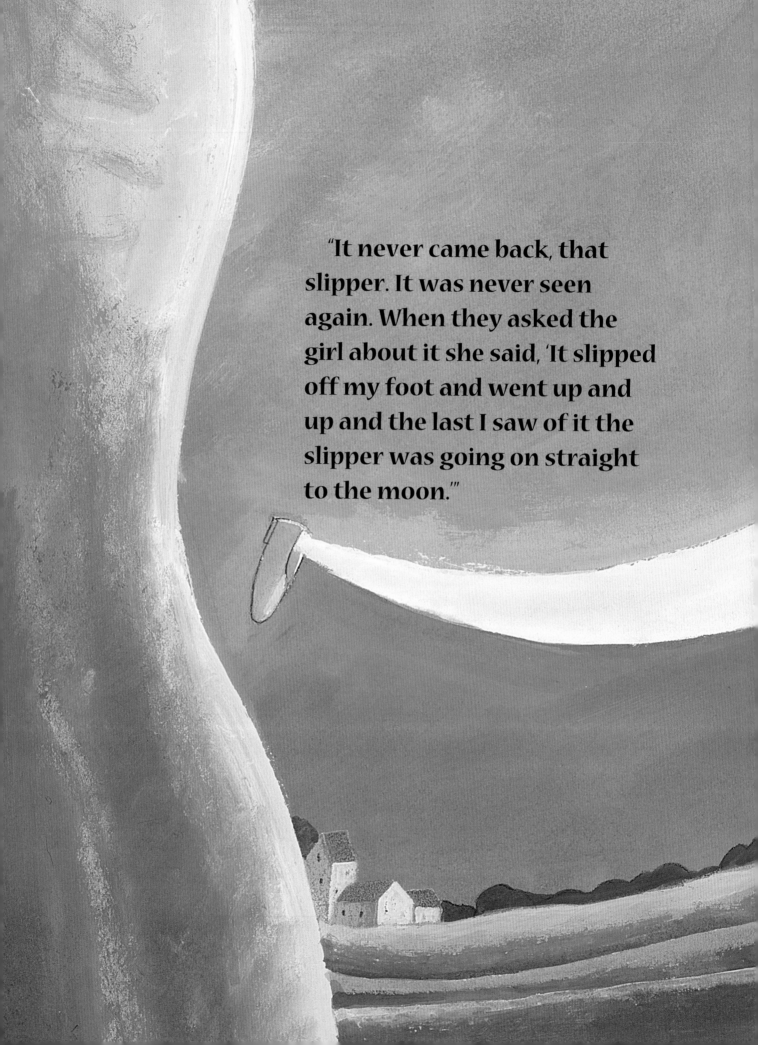

"It never came back, that slipper. It was never seen again. When they asked the girl about it she said, 'It slipped off my foot and went up and up and the last I saw of it the slipper was going on straight to the moon.'"

And these are the explanations why fathers and mothers in the Rootabaga Country say to their girls growing up, "Never kick a slipper at the moon if it is the time of the Dancing Slipper Moon when the ends of the moon look like the toe and the heel of a dancer's foot."

CARL SANDBURG was born in Galesburg, Illinois, in 1878 to poor Swedish immigrants. He left school at the age of thirteen to help support his family by working odd jobs and later joined the military and served in the Spanish-American War. Following the war he enrolled in Lombard College in Illinois; and while he never graduated, it was here that he began writing poetry. His first collection, *Reckless Ecstasy*, was published in 1904. However, it was more than ten years before he published again.

Sandburg wrote for years as a reporter and journalist, and worked for the Socialist-Democratic Party as well as the first Socialist mayor of Milwaukee. In 1916 he began contributing poems to the magazine *Poetry*. The publication of his *Chicago Poems* (1916), *Cornhuskers* (1918), and *Smoke and Steel* (1920) established his reputation as a poet of note, and he was recognized as a member of the Chicago literary renaissance.

Sandburg continued to write poetry, and his work became known for celebrating everyday life in America. His free verse writing reveled in the workings of American industry and agriculture, and revered the geography and people of the land. He looked for the beauty in ordinary things and common people, and in 1950 his *Complete Poems* was awarded a Pulitzer Prize.

In addition to poetry, Sandburg tried his hand at fiction, nonfiction, and children's literature. He penned the definitive biography of Abraham Lincoln, which took him more than thirty years to write and won him a Pulitzer Prize in 1939. His *Rootabaga Stories*, originally written for his daughters, are children's tales of utmost whimsy, depth, and imagination. Mr. Sandburg died in 1967 a world-renowned author and poet.

Harris County Public Library
Houston. Texas

Harris County Public Library
Houston. Texas